Adapted by
Tracey West

W9-BYF-656

SCHOLASTIC INC.

NEW YORK TORONTO LONDON AUCKLAND
SYDNEY MEXICO CITY NEW DELHI HONG KONG

ISBN-10: 0-545-16052-9
ISBN-13: 978-0-545-16052-0

CARTOON NETWORK, the logo, BEN 10 ALIEN SWARM and all related characters and elements are trademarks of and © 2009 Cartoon Network.
Published by Scholastic Inc.
SCHOLASTIC and associated logos are trademarks and/or registered trademarks of Scholastic Inc.

12 11 10 9 8 7 6 5 4 3 2 1   9 10 11 12 13 14/0

Designed by Rick DeMonico
Printed in the U.S.A.
First printing, September 2009

CHAPTER ONE

Vrooooooooooooooom . . .

The sound of a souped-up engine bounced off of the snowy hillsides surrounding the picturesque town of Bellwood. A bright green muscle car raced out of town, headed for a deserted mill in the middle of nowhere.

The car screeched to a stop outside the mill and the teenage driver got out. Kevin Levin's shaggy dark hair hung over his brown eyes. He looked tough in jeans, a black T-shirt, and a black short jacket. As he strode into the open space of the empty mill, a man with greasy hair approached him.

"What've you got for me, Fitz?" Kevin asked.

1

"I knew you'd be the guy to call on this, Kev, because it's big and I need to move it," Fitz said. He sounded nervous. "I figured you'd have the connections to—"

"Show me," Kevin said impatiently.

Fitz took out a cell phone and sent a text message. Seconds later, three Japanese motorcycles raced into the mill, surrounding Kevin and Fitz. They screeched to a stop. All three riders wore black leather pants and jackets with matching black helmets.

Two of the riders took off their helmets and approached Kevin. They were both young guys, and each was holding a sleek metal briefcase. The third rider hung back in the shadows.

"You the buyer?" one of the guys asked.

"Depends," Kevin replied. "What are you selling?"

"Alien technology," the guy said. "The good stuff."

He opened the lid of his briefcase and pulled out a clear glass tube secured with aluminum caps on each end. Inside the tube were what looked like a bunch of tiny microchips.

Kevin wasn't impressed. "Uh-huh. So? What are they?"

The tech dealer looked surprised. "You don't know?"

Kevin rolled his eyes. "*You* don't know, do you?" he said. "Is it a weapon? Does it fire? Can it blow stuff up? This is important information to a prospective buyer."

"It's alien technology, man," the guy said. "It's got to be worth some cash. You interested or not?"

"Chill," Kevin said. He reached out to examine the glass tube. "Let me talk to my partners."

Fitz looked more nervous than ever. "Partners? You didn't say anything about partners."

"Neither did you," Kevin said coolly.

Gwen Tennyson, a sixteen-year-old girl with long, red hair, stepped into the mill. Another figure walked behind her, a slim teenage boy wearing jeans and a black T-shirt. A green device that looked like a high-tech watch was strapped to his wrist.

Fitz went pale. "Uh, you're working with him?"

Ben Tennyson stepped forward. "Actually, I'm working with her," he said, nodding to Gwen. "Kevin doesn't really work. He just stands around flexing his muscles."

"How about I flex them on your face?" Kevin joked.

The second biker stepped up to Gwen and looked her over. Then he turned to Fitz. "Who are these jokers, man?"

"I can't tell you," Fitz said. "I'm just the middleman."

Gwen focused her intense green eyes on the biker. She wasn't the least bit intimidated. "We're just some regular old folks who are beginning to think this is a big fat waste of our time," she said.

Ben nodded at the chips in the tube. "What've we got?" he asked Kevin.

"Never seen anything like 'em," Kevin replied. "They're complex. Possibly self-replicating. Must be . . . grade nine tech at least."

The two biker guys looked impressed. Kevin knew what he was talking about.

Suddenly, the green device on Ben's wrist started flashing and making beeping noises. Ben messed around with some of the dials on it, but couldn't stop it.

"Whatever they are, they're screwing with the Omnitrix," Ben said, shaking his head.

"What's up with you guys? Never met dealers like you before," said the first biker.

The third biker finally spoke. Her voice was feminine but tough.

"You never met *anyone* like them before," she corrected him, "because they're not just black-market lowlifes like you. They're Plumbers."

The biker was confused. "You mean they're going to pay for this stuff by fixing my toilet?"

The girl biker took off her helmet. Dark hair spilled across her face.

"The Plumbers are a secret interplanetary security force. Saving the world so we don't have to." From the tone of her voice, it was clear she didn't like Plumbers very much.

Kevin tried to play it off. One of the important things about being a Plumber was keeping your secret job just that—a secret.

"Yeah, right. Of course. We're cops from outer space," he said. "Or maybe we're firemen from Atlantis."

Ben was curious. There was something familiar about the girl's voice. "How did you learn about these 'Plumbers' you think we are?"

"Everything I know about the Plumbers I learned the same way you did . . . Ben," the girl shot back.

Ben and his cousin Gwen exchanged glances. How did she know about the Plumbers? And how did she know Ben's name?

The girl finally stepped into the light. Her pretty face was marred by an angry scowl.

Ben's eyes went wide. "Elena?"

"No way," Gwen said.

"Who?" Kevin asked.

"Oh, you still remember me. I'm honored," Elena said sarcastically.

Kevin looked at Ben and Gwen. "Hello? Anybody want to toss me a clue about what's going on here?"

"Kevin, this is Elena Validus," Gwen said. Her voice was as frosty as the winter air. "She's a Plumber's kid, like us."

"Not like you, Gwen," Elena pointed out. "None of my ancestors were aliens. I don't have any cool powers to rely on."

"We hung out for a while back in the day," Ben told Kevin. "Then Elena's dad quit." He nodded to Elena. "Then you moved away and we haven't heard from you since."

Elena's eyes flashed with anger. "Is that what they told you? That my dad quit? Considering you've got more power than all of the Plumbers combined, you don't know much."

"Then why don't you tell me. What's going on?" Ben asked. "What are you doing here with these chips?"

"I'm here to find you," Elena said, and her voice softened a little. "The Plumbers don't exactly advertise. I need your help, Ben. It's my father. He's been abducted."

"Call the cops," Kevin suggested.

"They can't help," Elena snapped. "His disappearance is connected with these alien chips."

"We'll help you find him, Elena," Ben said earnestly. "You're a Plumber's kid and a friend."

"Am I, Ben? Really? Because life's been pretty hard for us the last three years, and I don't recall you ever looking us up," Elena said.

Before Ben could reply, a strange buzzing noise interrupted them.

"What is that?" Gwen asked. She looked at Elena accusingly. "Elena?"

"I don't know," Elena told her.

Inside the glass tube, the alien chips suddenly came to life. They buzzed and vibrated like a swarm of living insects. Together they threw themselves at the glass, trying to get out.

"It's a double cross," Kevin said.

Gwen grabbed her cousin's arm. "It's a trap, Ben."

"No, I swear it," Elena said. "I just wanted your help."

Fitz was sweating. "Well, I don't want to impose on your little dysfunction, so . . ."

Bam! The tube exploded. Chips flew in all directions. The two tech dealers dropped their briefcases and jumped back.

Bam! Bam! Bam! The other tubes exploded. Chips from each tube seemed to be drawn together. Soon there was one large swarm of chips buzzing above their heads like an alien rain cloud.

"Kevin, I think you were probably right about these not being ordinary computer chips," Ben quipped.

Above them, hidden in the rafters of the mill, a figure in a dark trenchcoat and hat watched the scene below. He raised his hands in the air in front of him like a symphony conductor. The swarm of alien chips moved when he moved. He was controlling them.

"Bring them back to ussssssss," the stranger hissed.

The mass of chips zoomed down like a swarm of bees.

They were under attack!

CHAPTER TWO

Thinking fast, Ben grabbed an old steel girder hanging from the ceiling. Wielding it like a baseball bat, he swung at the approaching swarm.

Whack! The blow sent many of the chips scattering—but now another swarm was headed for his cousin.

"Gwen!" he yelled.

Gwen did a quick backflip, springing out of the way. But the chips countered by forming a huge blob that was big enough to flatten her.

Gwen held out her hands, and a bubble of powerful pink energy shot out from them. The massive blob of chips crashed into Gwen's energy shield and shattered.

"Ben, I don't mean to backseat drive, but this might be a good time for the Omnitrix," Gwen called, her voice tense.

Ben looked down at the Omnitrix. Its lights were flashing out of control.

"Or not," Ben replied. "I think it's having a meltdown or something."

Another blob of chips had formed, ready to strike.

"Don't sweat it, dude," Kevin said. "If you can't handle it . . ." He touched one of the steel beams. Instantly, his whole body turned to steel. He kicked the blob, scattering the chips around the mill. The chips he'd destroyed fell to the floor like rain.

". . . I know someone who can!" Kevin bragged.

Ben snatched some of the dead chips from the ground. "They're not just chips," he reported. "It's some kind of alien nanotechnology."

"The attack is too organized," Gwen agreed. As she spoke, she sliced through clouds of chips with pink energy blades. "There must be some kind of intelligence behind it."

The last of the chips grouped together and flew at Elena and the two bikers. As she ducked out of the way,

Elena glanced up at the rafters. A look of shock crossed her face.

Ben followed her eyes. He spotted the shadowy figure moving his arms to control the chips.

"I don't know if he's intelligent, but I think we've found the puppeteer," Ben remarked.

The chips formed two large, razorlike blades. They zipped toward Ben, Gwen, and Kevin. As they flew, they sliced right through two steel columns. The columns toppled over, nearly taking out Elena and Fitz.

The two tech dealers jumped on their bikes and sped toward the mill entrance. A wall of chips blocked their way. The bikers quickly turned and crashed through a glass wall. They raced off into the distance.

"Too bad they had to leave before the main event," Ben said. He spun the dial on his Omnitrix. The device on Ben's wrist contained the DNA codes for aliens from all across the universe. With the Omnitrix, Ben could change into any of the forms he chose at will. And he knew just the right alien for this job. "Come on, Spidermonkey!"

A small hologram of Spidermonkey beamed from the Omnitrix. Ben slammed on the device's dial. Green light covered his body as he transformed . . . into Big Chill!

The Omnitrix had messed up—but why?

Big Chill had a blue humanoid body, a face like an insect, and large wings.

"This is so not Spidermonkey," Ben said in Big Chill's raspy voice.

"Less talking, more freezing," Kevin called out.

Big Chill flew at the last swarm of chips. They passed right through his ghostly form and instantly froze. The chips that survived tried to pull together for another attack, but they shattered against one another.

The chips rose overhead and formed a swirling tornado. Gwen fired a round of energy blasts at them. "A little help here?"

Big Chill flew toward the spiral of chips, blasting them with a powerful shot of freezing breath. This time, the frozen tornado shattered completely. Dead chips rained down on the mill floor.

"Thanks," Elena said.

"No problem," Big Chill replied.

The few chips that survived the blast flew up to the rafters. The figure in the trenchcoat was still there, watching them.

"Who is that, Elena?" Kevin asked.

"Who's controlling all this?" Gwen wondered.

"I . . . don't know," Elena said hesitantly.

"Then let's find out," Big Chill said.

He zoomed up to the rafters and fired a freezing blast at the mysterious figure. The rafter exploded and the figure jumped off, hurling a ball of alien chips at Big Chill.

Big Chill ducked, and the ball landed on the ground right in front of Gwen.

Boom! Gwen went flying backward.

"Gwen!" Kevin ran to her and cradled her in his arms.

Big Chill morphed back into Ben. He approached his cousin.

"Gwen, you okay?"

Gwen sat up. "Yeah, I'm fine."

"Who is that guy?" Kevin asked.

The mysterious figure was nowhere to be seen. Above them, a small cloud of chips exited through the open skylight.

"I think you mean, who *was* he?" Ben replied. Then he turned, panicked. "Elena!"

But there was no sign of Elena either.

"If you're looking for your girlfriend, I think your personal charm was too much for her," Kevin said.

"Kevin's right," Gwen said. "She set us up."

"Did she?" Ben wondered. "I'm not so sure."

CHAPTER THREE

Kevin pulled the car in front of Bellwood Auto Shop. He, Gwen, and Ben climbed out of the car.

Ben was examining the Omnitrix.

"This whole thing is wrong from top to bottom," he said.

"Yeah, starting with that crazy biker–babe girlfriend of yours," Kevin added.

"Elena was not my *girlfriend*, Kevin," Ben told him. "We were like, thirteen."

"Her story doesn't add up, Ben," Gwen said. She and Elena had never gotten along. "Why sell alien tech on the black market just to find the Plumbers when her father used to be one?"

Ben looked thoughtful. "She said that something happened with her dad back when they lived here and we weren't told the truth about it. If that's the case, Grandpa Max has some serious explaining to do."

They walked inside the auto shop. The noisy sound of drills and lifts came from the auto repair bays attached to the main office. Boxes of auto parts were stacked on big shelves behind the counter. Big Ed, the shop owner, was talking to a pretty teenage girl and her father.

"Sorry, Mr. Suda," Big Ed was saying. "That old girl needs new pistons and there's no getting around it."

He nodded when the kids entered. "Hey guys."

"Gotta grab something outta the back, Ed," Kevin said.

Ed winked and nodded. The girl smiled at Ben.

"You going to the game tomorrow, Ben?" she asked.

"Hope so, Molly," Ben told her. "Just got hit with some serious, uh, homework."

He and Gwen walked through a doorway past the counter. Kevin stopped at the soda machine to get a drink.

"You know Benjie," Kevin said to Molly. "All work and no play."

He caught up to Ben and Gwen. They headed down a hallway to a door marked "Office." As Ben unlocked it, Gwen examined some of the dead alien chips in her palm.

"I'm really looking forward to getting this under a scanner," she said.

"I'm really looking forward to hunting down that creepazoid and his army of flying chips," Ben added.

He opened the door. There was no office behind it. Instead, they stepped inside a giant industrial elevator.

"You mean the chips your gal pal *illegally* had in her possession?" Kevin asked.

"All right, Kev, I think he gets it," Gwen said.

Kevin loudly popped open his soda and started to slurp it down.

Ben shook his head. "I have no clue what you see in him," he told Gwen.

The elevator took them down to the secret Plumbers' comm center and lab hidden below the auto shop. Elena might not have liked the Plumbers, but her description of them was pretty accurate. Plumbers were members of an intergalactic police force charged with keeping bad guys under control—and there were plenty of bad guys in the universe.

An effort that big needed a lot of technology to work, and the Plumbers' lab was full of it.

"Systems up," Ben said loudly.

At the sound of his voice, the room powered up. Lights flashed on, computers hummed, and data screens glowed.

"Ben, did you ask Grandpa Max if we could use the comm center?" Gwen asked.

"No time for that," Ben replied. "You want to start solving this thing, or go looking for a permission slip?"

Gwen looked at Kevin. He shrugged. Ben had a point.

Gwen sat down at one of the work stations and got to work analyzing the dead chips. The results popped up on a line of computer monitors.

"Austenitic, ferritic, and martensitic microstructure," Gwen read. "Alien compositional methods. Both organic and inorganic materials."

"Gwen, you are a credit to the science club," Ben said.

Kevin studied a magnified chip on one of the screens. "Never seen anything like this. It's tech, but it's also a carbon-based life form."

"So they're alive," Ben realized.

"They were. Kind of," Kevin said. "Now they're in alien chip heaven."

"Let me see if I can trace where they came from," Gwen said.

Gwen had powers that came from her alien grandmother, who was an Anodite, a being of pure energy. One of her powers was the ability to track where things came from based on their energy signatures.

Gwen held her hands above a pile of the dead chips and concentrated. Her hands glowed with pink light as she tried to run an energy trace on the chips.

After a moment, Gwen sighed. "Nothing. They're completely inert. I can't pick up any energy signature. What now?"

"Well . . . maybe I can jump-start an energy pulse from this slag," Kevin said reluctantly, "but it would take forever and be a total pain in the—"

He stopped when he saw Gwen's smile. He had a hard time saying no to her. "Okay. I'll get right on it."

"Or we could just find Elena and ask her where these came from," Ben suggested.

"What makes you think she would tell you the truth?" Gwen asked. "She could have set us up."

"She's one of us," Ben insisted.

"She *was* one of us," Gwen pointed out. "You have no idea who she is now. You can't trust her."

Ben was getting a little tired of hearing he couldn't trust Elena. She had been a good friend just a few years ago. Could she really have changed that much?

"Evidently, I can't trust anyone," Ben muttered. "I can't even trust Grandpa Max."

"Can't trust me to what?"

Ben turned to see Grandpa Max had entered the lab, carrying a bowl of soup.

"We can't trust you to make soup without putting baked moss or lizard gizzards in it," Gwen said quickly.

"Hmm, that sounds like a pretty good combo," Max said. He was completely serious, too. He took a sip of his soup.

Grandpa Max had gray streaks in his hair, but looked stronger than men half his age. A longtime Plumber, Grandpa Max had always been there for Ben—both before and after he became linked with the Omnitrix.

"So what are you guys doing down in the hole on off hours?" he asked.

"We had a little situation," Kevin explained.

Max wandered over to the monitors and stopped in front of the magnified view of one of the chips.

"What is that?" he asked. "Seems familiar. I've seen this somewhere before."

"You have? Where?" Gwen asked.

"Max, there's something you need to explain," Ben began. "I want to know what happened—"

Beep! Beep! Beep!

An alarm went off, and a red warning light flashed on the ceiling.

"Sounds like we have an uninvited guest," Max said. "Ben, punch up a tracker on the complex."

"No need, Grandpa," Gwen said. Her eyes were glowing pink. "I've got 'em."

Gwen slowly walked out of the lab, followed by the others. She walked down a hallway and stopped.

"They're in Max's office," she said.

"They better not touch my model train collection," Max grumbled. "I just painted the caboose."

They rushed through the office door. Just about every inch of Max's office was crammed with furniture, computer equipment, and strange pieces of alien tech.

Gwen pointed to a dark corner of the office. Something moved behind a metal rack. Grandpa Max took a laser weapon from his belt and fired it up. Kevin touched a metal shelf and turned both of his arms into armor. Gwen glowed with alien energy. If there was a dangerous alien waiting there, they would be ready for it.

"Whoever you are, you picked the wrong place to break into," Kevin called out. "You're going to be one fried, roasted, and baked . . ."

Elena stepped out from behind the rack.

". . . babe?" Kevin finished.

Ben pushed down the barrel of Max's weapon.

"It's okay, Max. You probably don't recognize her, she's . . ."

Max's face turned to an icy mask. "It's *not* okay. It's a Validus."

He glared at Elena. "How did you get in here?"

Elena held up the key to the back office.

"Time to get Big Ed some glasses," Kevin noted.

"Been a long time, Mr. Tennyson," Elena said.

Gwen stopped glowing. Kevin's arms turned back to normal.

"You shouldn't have come here, Elena," Max said coldly.

"Max, Elena was the one who set up the sale of those weird chips," Gwen said.

"Of course," Max said. "I knew I'd seen them before." He nodded to Elena. "Time for you to go."

"Mr. Tennyson, I had to do that," Elena explained. "I need help. And it was the only way I could think of to get it."

She didn't look so tough anymore, Ben realized. He was convinced—she really did need help.

But Max wasn't moved. "You know the rules. You need to go. Now."

"It's my father," Elena pleaded. "He's been kidnapped. By whoever . . . or whatever . . . made those chips. I knew that only the Plumbers could help."

Max turned to Kevin and Gwen. "Get her out of here."

"You're not serious!" Ben protested. "She needs help."

"That's an order!" Max said firmly.

Kevin and Gwen each held one of Elena's arms and escorted her to the door.

"Sorry, you heard the man," Kevin told her.

"Come on, Elena," Gwen said. "I don't know what's going on, but he means it."

Elena yanked her arm free from Gwen's hand. "Then I'll *tell* you what's going on, Gwen. Your sweet old grandpa turned his back on us three years ago. Threw us out in the street when we needed his help, and lied to you both to cover his tracks. Now my father has ended up in serious trouble and Max still won't help us."

"Is this true?" Ben asked. He turned to his grandfather. "Can't we just talk to her?'

"No, Ben," Max said. "Everything she would say would be a lie. Kevin?"

Kevin moved Elena toward the door.

Ben was stunned. How could they be treating her like this?

"Thanks for the help. You're real heroes," Elena said, her voice sharp. "And Ben . . . thanks for being a *real* friend."

CHAPTER FOUR

Kevin led Elena out the door. Ben turned to his grandfather.

"What's wrong with you?" he asked.

"There's nothing wrong with me," Max replied. "But there's something very wrong with *her*. She's Victor Validus's daughter."

"Okay, I'm sufficiently stumped," Gwen said. "What's going on here?"

Max sat down at his computer terminal. He switched on the monitor and began typing into his keyboard. The image of a man with dark hair, brown eyes, and a thin face appeared on the screen.

"Victor Validus was the best Plumber I ever trained," Max began. "We stopped more than our share of invasions. Stopped the Earth from blowing up. Good times. I trusted Vic with my life. He was a good friend and a great Plumber . . . until he betrayed us."

A stamp of big red letters flashed across Victor's face on the screen: "Decommissioned Without Honor."

"What?" Ben couldn't believe it.

"Caught him stealing alien technology from our vault," Max said darkly. "Tech he had sworn to protect the Earth from. He was dishonorably discharged. A traitor."

Kevin entered the room. "The traitor's daughter has left the building," he reported.

"What did he steal?" Gwen asked.

"The same stuff you found Elena dealing," Max replied. He shut off the screen. "You still think she's the girl you knew, Ben?"

"She told the truth about one thing," Ben pointed out. "You lied to us."

"I did that for your own good," Max said gruffly. "You were too young to understand."

"I still don't understand," Ben said. He loved his grandfather, but he was getting angrier by the minute. "You can't judge her by what her father did!"

"Stay away from her, Ben," Max warned. "The Validus family has been blacklisted. There is to be no Plumber interaction with them."

Ben paced the floor. "That's the way you see it. Way I see it, a friend is in trouble, and she's the best link we have to those chips and the freak controlling them. A whole lot more people could end up in trouble besides Elena and her father!"

Max stood up. "That's why we're gonna analyze the chips and deal with this crisis by the book," he said firmly. "I'm not putting out a high alert with nothing but that girl's word to go on. And that's my decision to make."

Ben locked eyes with his grandfather, then shook his head.

"Well, that's the wrong decision," he said. "I'm sorry, Max. I'm not following your order."

Ben walked toward the door. Gwen stared at him, stunned.

"Ben, you can't break Plumber ranks!" she cried. She turned to Max. "You can't let him do this!"

Max looked sad. "It's not up to me, Gwen. He's made his choice."

Ben paused in front of Kevin, hoping his friend would join him. But Kevin shook his head.

"Someone's gotta stay here and look after the old man," Kevin said.

Ben nodded. He understood.

"Kevin, stop him!" Gwen cried.

Ben stopped. "Don't worry," he told his cousin. "I can handle myself."

Ben knew that turning his back on the Plumbers and disobeying Max was a big deal. But he just couldn't believe that Elena was some kind of criminal. She needed help. If Max wouldn't help her, then it was up to him.

He left Max's office and didn't look back.

As the sun set, Elena roared through Bellwood on her motorcycle. Another bike pulled out of a side street, zipped in front of her, and pulled to a hard ninety-degree stop, blocking her path. The rider wore a green jacket with the number ten on it—Ben's trademark.

Elena expertly skidded to a halt and took off her helmet.

"What do you want?" she asked angrily.

Ben removed his helmet, too. "Same thing as you. I want to help you find him."

A happy look crossed Elena's face, but she quickly covered it up with her usual tough stare. "What about your gramps?" she asked.

"Not too thrilled about it," Ben replied.

"And you're helping me anyway."

Ben shrugged. Elena nodded toward his motorcycle.

"Nice bike."

"It's Max's really," Ben admitted, and Elena raised an eyebrow. "Can't get any angrier with me than he is already."

"I'm sorry. That's my fault," Elena said, and she looked like she meant it.

"No, it's his," Ben replied. "Let's find your dad. First stop, wherever you got your hands on those chips."

He put his helmet back on and revved up the bike. Elena did the same. Together, they zoomed away.

CHAPTER FIVE

Inside Plumbers' headquarters, a dim light burned in Max's office. Gwen stepped inside.

"Grandpa?"

But Kevin was sitting at Max's desk, working on the computer.

"You find your wayward cousin?" he asked.

"He'll be back," Gwen replied. "Alone, hopefully."

"What's the 411 on those two?"

"Elena was Ben's first crush," Gwen explained. "She was the only girl on his soccer team back in middle school. Ben couldn't kick a ball in a straight line when she was around. He was really bummed out after she moved away."

"Great. So now it's puppy love?" Kevin asked.

"Cousin Ben is growing up," Gwen said. "Had to happen sometime."

"I'll believe that when I see it," Kevin joked.

Gwen leaned over his shoulder. "Kevin, what are you doing here in Max's office?"

"I wanted to know what intel we already had on those chips," he replied. "If Validus took them from the vault, they should be in the system."

"And?"

"All the files are sealed," Kevin reported.

"Then you should just ask Max to—"

"Tried that," Kevin interrupted her. "He was not open to discussion."

Gwen's eyes widened. "So you just came in here and opened his personal files?" she asked accusingly. Then her tone changed. "What do they say?"

"They're sort of locked," Kevin said. "I couldn't figure out the password."

"That would be a huge violation of trust," Gwen said.

"And regulations," Kevin added. He knew Gwen didn't like to break the rules—unless there was a good reason. He'd just have to give her one.

"So I guess Ben really is on his own," Kevin said casually. "I'm sure he'll be fine. I mean, he's all grown-up now and everything."

Gwen had been worried about Ben all day. She leaned over the computer.

"Break the code," she said.

Kevin smiled and started typing.

A man in a long trenchcoat and hat—the same man from the rooftop of the old mill—walked down a dark alley. The alien chips swirled around his tattered coat as he walked, muttering to himself.

"No, no, do not worry. Our work advances nicely. . . . Yes, yes we have completed our tests. Please, we must know. Is it time?"

Two rough-looking guys stepped out of the shadows in front of him.

"Oh yeah pal, it's time," said the first guy. "Time for you to give us your money."

The man kept on walking, acting like he didn't see them. The thugs got annoyed.

"Hey, we're talking to you, loony toon," the second guy called out angrily. "Don't you know this is a bad part of town? You shouldn't be out walking alone."

The man stopped and raised his head. The streetlight illuminated his face — the face of Victor Validus, Elena's father! But he looked different from the picture on Max's computer screen. His face was sunken and hollow, and his skin was dry and flaky. Dark scales resembling the alien chips speckled his skin.

Victor eyed the two would-be thieves and laughed. It was an eerie sound, part human, part machine.

"Alone?" Victor said, and it sounded like a hundred voices were speaking from inside him. "We are not alone. We are never alone. . . ."

"Your wallet, fool!" barked the first thug.

"We offer you so much more than money," Victor told them. "We offer you a new life!"

A swarm of chips swirled out from under his coat and descended on the surprised criminals. One of the chips landed on the first guy's neck and buried itself in his skin.

"Join usssss," Victor hissed. "Help usssss. Rule with usssss!"

As Victor's voice swelled, the swarm began to buzz. The thugs screamed as the chips surrounded them, engulfing them.

Victor turned and walked away. A few moments later, the chips followed.

The thugs slowly rose from the ground and lumbered after Victor and the chips. They looked like zombies. A shaft of light shone on their expressionless faces, revealing a strange force moving behind their eyes. . . .

CHAPTER SIX

Ben and Elena rode their motorcycles down the streets of a nearby city. They roared past office buildings and restaurants. Soon the streets became narrower and dirtier. The buildings looked run-down, with broken windows and graffiti on the walls. Trash spilled from overturned garbage cans.

The two teens pulled up in front of an old stone building with crumbling walls. A dim streetlamp scattered light across the door through a broken glass globe.

"What is this place?" Ben asked.

"Used to be city hall, way back in the day," Elena explained. "My dad started acting really weird a couple of months ago. I followed him one night. Here."

"Hanging around here certainly classifies as 'weird,'" Ben agreed.

They climbed off of their bikes and walked toward the door. They didn't see him, but Victor Validus was watching them from a window on the second floor.

"That's a good girl," he whispered. "Bring him right to us. . . . He can't help you. . . ."

Ben stepped into the building and hesitated at the sight of the dust and cobwebs in the deserted space.

"What was he doing in here? Racing cockroaches?" Ben joked.

"He has a kind of laboratory set up," Elena told him, as she led him to a staircase in the center of the room. "Whatever he was working on, he didn't want me involved. Then he stopped coming home at all."

Ben understood how hard that must have been for Elena—to suddenly be left all alone. More than ever, he knew that helping her was the right decision. He followed her up to the second floor.

Meanwhile, Victor Validus was outside the building at a loading dock in the back. An eighteen-wheeler was backed up to the dock, and a crew of zombie-like workers were loading crates into the truck under Victor's direction. They worked swiftly, without saying a word.

Suddenly, Victor gazed up at the building's second floor. Every worker's head turned at the same time. Then they looked back to Victor, who nodded. He didn't need to speak — they understood.

Victor climbed into the truck. Several of the workers headed back into the building, ready to do their master's bidding.

Inside, Ben and Elena explored Victor's lab. A mess of files, papers, and lab equipment was scattered on the floor. A few rickety tables and desks had their drawers turned upside down.

"Someone's been here, taking things," Elena guessed.

"Or looking for things," Ben said. "What was your dad doing?"

"He was studying the chips," Elena replied.

Ben shook his head. "Boy, when he takes up a hobby, he doesn't mess around."

He searched through the clutter. Alien symbols were scrawled on some of the papers; on others, he saw drawings of the chips, charts, and long columns of numbers.

"Elena, these notes. He wasn't studying the chips," Ben realized. "He was upgrading them. *Developing* them. Look at this. Man, your dad's really crazy."

Elena got defensive. "You're wrong. He's a brilliant man. He just became . . . possessed by his work."

Ben moved to a desk, where he spotted a framed photo of Elena and her dad. They both looked normal and happy. The man in the photo didn't look like someone capable of creating the frenzied mess in the lab.

"Why did he become possessed?" Ben asked.

"He said these things pose some kind of threat," Elena explained. "The Plumbers didn't believe him. So he took them. Now they won't lift a finger to help him."

"Yeah, well, Max is kind of a stickler for the Plumber rule book," Ben said.

Elena rummaged through the drawers of a metal file cabinet. "This is where I found those chips and the storage canisters. There were more. . . ."

But the drawers were empty. Elena looked through the other cabinets in the room and found nothing.

"They were all over the place. I swear it," she said.

Ben picked up a stack of papers. As he leafed through them, he realized they were invoices from an overnight delivery service — the Ship-It company.

"Looks like your dad had some business with Ship-It," Ben remarked. "You think he could have sent the chips off somewhere?"

Elena shrugged. Ben stuffed the invoices into his pocket.

"Well, whoever has your dad wanted those chips. Like that freaky guy we saw before. You know who he is?" Ben asked.

Elena looked away nervously. "I have no idea. I just want to get my father back, Ben."

"We'll get him. I promise," Ben assured her.

Elena gasped. When Ben looked up at her, he realized she was staring at something just behind him. He turned to see a small group of people standing there. They were all different—a guy in a suit, a woman in a nurse's uniform, another dude in a blue jumpsuit—but they all had the same weird, zombie-like look in their eyes.

"Who are you? What do you want?" Ben asked. Something wasn't right.

"We want to help . . . you," said the guy in the suit in a creepy voice.

The people surrounded Ben and Elena.

"No thanks. I'm good. Just browsing," Ben said casually. Then he whispered to Elena, "Check out their eyes."

He grabbed a desk lamp and shone it on their faces. The light reflected off the metal alien chips moving behind their eyeballs. More chips were crawling under the skin of their arms and faces.

"The chips! They're infected!" Elena cried. "They're being controlled."

The nurse zombie slowly moved toward them. "We want you to meet the queen."

Ben and Elena slowly took a step backward.

"And we would love to do that, but all that bowing and curtsying? I don't think so," Ben said.

The zombies advanced on them. More were lumbering up the stairs.

"Too many of them," Ben said. Then he realized something. "Like they were expecting us. Like this was a trap."

A look of suspicion crossed his face. Was Max right about Elena after all?

Ben didn't even have to ask the question. "No. I swear," Elena told him.

The zombies had them backed up against a wall. Ben pulled up his sleeve and turned the dial on the Omnitrix. "Looks like we could use a little help . . . "

The Omnitrix beeped and flashed. Every time he turned the dial, half-formed shapes appeared instead of the full holographic alien forms he could turn into.

". . . from a squiggly static blob," Ben finished. "Not good."

He quickly scanned the room. There had to be another option. Then he saw it—a metal door just a few feet away.

"Fire escape! Run!" Ben shouted.

CHAPTER SEVEN

They raced for the fire escape door. Elena flung it open—to reveal a zombie on the other side.

Bam! Ben surprised him with a punch. The zombie doubled over, and Elena hurled him off of the fire escape rail.

They bounded down the stairs. The zombies followed right behind him. When they reached the last metal step, they jumped down to the street and raced to the front of the building, where their bikes were.

"No!" Elena yelled.

A small army of zombies circled their bikes. They looked tougher than the ones inside the building. These zombies were a mass of leather jackets, tattoos, and piercings.

The zombies spotted Ben and Elena and began shuffling toward them.

"What do we do?" Elena asked.

Ben glanced at his Omnitrix, which was still beeping and flashing out of control.

"Okay, I think I get it," he said, thinking out loud. "When the Omnitrix encounters new forms of life, it scans and reconstitutes their DNA. So if these chips are actually alive, like some form of techno-organic interface, then the watch would go into overdrive to scan them, right?"

"Can we have this pop quiz some other time?" Elena asked nervously.

"Maybe I can redirect the scan back at the chips," Ben replied calmly. "If I can just boost the power . . ."

He quickly adjusted some of the controls on the Omnitrix. Behind them, the zombies climbed off the fire escape. In moments, Ben and Elena would be surrounded by zombies on all sides.

"Got it!" Ben cried.

He slammed the Omnitrix. A green, rippling pulse radiated from the device. There was a deafening sound. The blast hit the zombies, and they went flying backward.

"Hey! Not bad," Ben remarked.

But the zombies recovered quickly and started to get back on their feet.

"Not great, either," Elena pointed out. "Let's go!"

They scrambled onto their bikes and revved their engines. As they sped off, a zombie dove into Elena's path. She swerved to avoid it, but she moved too sharply and too quickly.

Elena cried out as her bike tipped over, sending her sprawling on the ground. The zombies headed for her.

"Ben!" she yelled.

Ben spun into a quick 180-degree turn. He gunned it, heading straight through the crowd of zombies.

He rode up to Elena and reached out, grabbing her arm and pulling her onto the bike behind him. She wrapped her arms around him and they blasted away, leaving the zombies in the dust.

Ben didn't stop until the zombies were a safe distance behind them. He and Elena looked back at the abandoned city hall.

"Thanks," Elena said. "You're pretty good on this thing. How long have you been riding it?"

"Oh, about two hours," Ben replied.

"What do we do now?" Elena asked.

"We visit the Ship-It center and find out what your dad was up to," Ben told her. "Maybe we even find your dad."

Elena frowned. "Whatever he sent is long gone now."

Ben dug into his pocket and pulled out one of the invoices he had found. "Sure about that?"

Elena took it from him. "This is dated today."

"I thought you said he'd been missing for weeks?" Ben asked.

Elena looked away from him. "He has!" she insisted. "It can't be my dad. You believe me, don't you?"

"I believe it," Ben said. "We'll find something at Ship-It."

Ben revved the bike, and they raced off into the night.

Back in Plumbers HQ, Kevin had managed to break into Max's files. He and Gwen watched an old video interrogation on one of the computer monitors. Max was questioning a younger, normal-looking Victor Validus.

"Who were you going to sell the chips to, Victor?" Max asked angrily.

"I keep telling you! I had to take them," Victor said desperately. "It was for research! Those chips, they're a threat! They're *planning* something."

Max leaned over and glared at Victor. "You're lying. They're dead. The lab boys say they're nothing but alien tech computer chips. No threat at all. Now, who's your buyer?"

Victor ran a hand through his hair. "The hive wants us! All of us! I can't explain it, but it's true! Max, they're coming for us. They're coming for us all!"

Kevin turned down the sound. "Your gramps has a great bedside manner there, Gwen."

"Validus was like his prize pupil. Grandpa Max really felt betrayed. I wonder if . . ." Gwen's voice trailed off.

Kevin finished her thought. "You think maybe Max's getting stabbed in the back is keeping him from seeing straight. That would make . . ."

". . . Ben right," Gwen said, nodding.

"That's a scary thought," Kevin admitted. "And not just because I hate it when he's right."

Gwen started to pace back and forth, her mind

racing. "So what if this loony isn't loony? What if the chips weren't dead?"

"Like some kind of species of insect that can remain dormant for decades," Kevin said. Gwen looked at him, surprised. "Learned that off the Science Channel."

"Your depth of knowledge astounds," Gwen teased. "Have any luck getting a trace off their energy signature?"

Kevin started flipping switches. "Your wish was my headache-inducing project," he said.

A map of the Bellwood area appeared on the largest screen in the room. Clusters of red dots were scattered in different locations all over the map.

"They're showing up in a hundred mile radius," he explained.

"Kevin, you did it!" Gwen leaned down and kissed him on the cheek. Then she started typing at a break-neck pace.

Kevin leaned back in his chair. "The cheek. I find all the big, bad alien chips and I get a kiss on the cheek," he muttered.

Gwen punched him playfully on the arm. Then she went back to the keyboard and zoomed in on an area of the map. It was covered with a thick cluster of dots.

"Check it out. The greatest concentration of chips is over here," she said.

Kevin clicked on the spot, and the logo for the Ship-It center popped up on the screen.

"It's a Ship-It distribution center," he said.

"That's only about an hour from here," Gwen said. "Are you thinking what I'm thinking?"

"That we're officially going against orders and are no better than Ben?" Kevin said.

Gwen sighed. "You had to mention it."

An hour later, Kevin and Gwen reached the distribution center. It was a huge, multilevel warehouse with trucking bays on three sides. It was dark out, and the place looked deserted.

The locked door was no problem for Kevin. He touched a rock, transforming his fist into solid stone.

Bam! He punched right through the lock on the door, and it swung in.

"Come on. It's open," he whispered to Gwen.

Gwen glanced at the shattered lock on the floor. "It's open, huh?"

Kevin grinned. "It's open now."

They switched on their flashlights and scanned the warehouse. The large space was filled with row after row of empty shelves.

"Remind me again why we drove all the way out here?" Kevin asked.

Gwen held out her right hand. It glowed softly as she drew in energy from the space.

"They were here, Kev. We're too late."

She walked through a door into a row of offices adjacent to the main warehouse space.

Kevin held up his right hand. Of course, nothing happened. "Yeah, sure. That's what I get, too," he said.

Kevin stepped into the dark, eerie hallway. The offices all looked empty. "Man, there's *nothing* here anymore," he remarked.

Then Gwen called out. "There's *something*! Check it out!"

Kevin followed the sound of her voice and found her in an office, rifling through a stack of papers.

"London, Paris, Shanghai. These orders originated from this location and are headed all over the world," Gwen reported. "Literally. Air, sea, by every means they have."

Kevin opened a file cabinet drawer stuffed with papers. "There must be thousands of crate orders. Maybe a hundred thousand."

Gwen frowned. "Kevin, what do you think it means?"

"It means we're at least one step behind something disturbingly huge," Kevin replied.

"May I help you?"

The inhuman voice startled them both. They turned to see a skinny guy wearing a blue, striped shirt with the Ship-It logo on the pocket. He stared at them blankly from a desk that had been empty just moments before. Where had he come from?

"Um, hi," Gwen said. "We just had a few questions."

"Ship-It is closed right now," the man said in a robotic voice. "Please return during regular business hours."

"And what are you doing here? In the dark?" Gwen asked suspiciously.

"We are workers," the skinny clerk said. "We live to obey."

"You must be Employee of the Month," Kevin quipped.

A shaft of light from Kevin's flashlight reflected off of the clerk's eyes. At the same moment, Gwen and Kevin saw the alien chips moving behind them.

Gwen gave Kevin a small nod. "Listen, mister," Gwen said carefully. "We need to take some of these documents with us for a little school project. I'll bring them right back after we turn in our report, okay?"

"No. You will remain," the clerk said firmly. "You will join us."

Kevin reached over the counter and grabbed the guy's shirt. "I'm going to have to insist," he threatened.

"Your desires are irrelevant. The queen's will supercedes all," the clerk replied.

Kevin touched the wood desk, and his arm transformed into solid wood. He pounded the zombie clerk, sending him flying through the plate glass office window.

Kevin and Gwen charged toward the door. They raced out of the warehouse and jumped into Kevin's car.

As Kevin slammed the door behind them, Gwen glanced behind her and saw the clerk walking toward them. He raised his hands in the air.

"What's that weirdo doing?" she asked.

Kevin looked back. "Don't know. Praying to the great god of bubble wrap?"

"Kevin!" Gwen shouted.

Kevin turned. A swarm of alien chips was diving out of the sky, heading straight for the car.

"Okay, these chips are now officially an issue," he said.

The chips joined together to form hundreds of perfect metal spheres the size of baseballs.

"That's new," Gwen realized. "They couldn't form solid shapes before. The chips must be learning."

Bam! Bam! Bam!

The metal chip balls smacked into the car. They hit the windshield, cracking the glass.

"Not the glass! That's custom!" Kevin yelled.

"Let's get out of here!" Gwen cried.

CHAPTER EIGHT

The metal spheres floated up and grouped together again, ready for another attack. Kevin started the engine and peeled away from the warehouse. Behind them, the zombie clerk called out, "Thank you for using Ship-It!"

Kevin raced out of the parking lot and drove down a street. Gwen pointed up ahead.

"Looks like we have company."

The alien chips had re-formed. Now two giant metal spheres the size of cars rolled down the street, headed right for them! Kevin cut the wheel, swerving to avoid one, then the other.

"You should teach a driving class," Gwen said.

Kevin grinned. "Defensive drivers are the best drivers."

Gwen checked the rearview mirror. The two spheres had re-formed into three spheres. Three spheres would be much harder for Kevin to dodge.

"I think they're getting smarter," Gwen said nervously.

"Then so will we."

Kevin made a sharp turn and sped toward a service tunnel underneath an overpass. It was just wide enough for his car—but not wide enough for the spheres.

But Gwen was right. The chips were getting smarter. The three big spheres broke up into a bunch of smaller spheres. Sharp spikes sprouted around their edges. They plowed into the tunnel, tearing up asphalt as they chased after Kevin's car.

"You get an 'E' for effort," Gwen joked.

"Okay, so we gotta be smarter *and* faster," Kevin said.

He gunned the engine and emerged from the tunnel, narrowly missing another car. The spheres quickly adapted, flattening themselves to zoom under the car. They re-formed and began their pursuit again.

On a nearby street, Ben pulled Max's motorcycle to a stop. He checked the GPS navigator on his phone.

"The Ship-It office is up here," he told Elena.

Just then, the distinctive roar of an engine broke the silence.

"What was that?" Elena asked.

"The most obnoxious muscle car in the world," Ben replied. "We're making a detour."

As Ben and Elena raced toward the sound of his car, Kevin turned down a long, straight stretch of road. He flipped a switch on the dash, and the alien tech he had installed in the car kicked in. His car shot down the straightaway like a rocket. But it wasn't fast enough.

The spheres pulled up on either side of Kevin, ripping into the side of the car with their spikes. Then they lifted the car into the air, flipping it over!

"Hang on!" Kevin yelled.

CRASH! The car landed upside down. Kevin and Gwen climbed out of the windows as the spheres streaked past them.

"You okay?" Kevin asked.

Gwen gave a weak smile. "It hurts when I laugh, but I don't think that'll be a problem."

Kevin looked angry. "I don't know who's behind all this, but they're gonna fix my car."

They looked around. There was no sign of the spheres. Everything was quiet.

"You think they gave up?" Kevin asked.

"Maybe they just wanted to scare us," Gwen guessed.

Kevin looked up. "Well, they succeeded. I'm scared."

An enormous metal ball rose up from the overpass above them. It was as big as a house. As Gwen and Kevin watched in horrified amazement, long, sharp spikes popped out all over its surface.

The sphere rolled off of the overpass, smashing into the ground. It rolled toward Gwen and Kevin.

Gwen quickly raised her arms and hurled blasts of pink energy at the ball, but it didn't slow down.

There was nowhere to run. Kevin touched his car, then stepped in front of Gwen.

Ben and Elena sped up just as the ball advanced on Kevin and Gwen. Ben steered with one hand as he tried to dial up an alien form on the Omnitrix. The crazy beeping and flashing had finally stopped. Ben whipped off his helmet.

"It's working!" he yelled to Elena. "Take over!"

"Are you crazy?" Elena asked. "Don't even—"

Ben jumped off of the bike, hitting the Omnitrix at the same time. He sailed through the air, transforming into Humungousaur! The huge, dinosaur-like alien landed on two feet in front of the giant alien sphere. The ground shook beneath his massive form.

"Humungousaur!" he roared.

Elena skidded to a stop in front of Kevin and Gwen.

"Nice timing," Kevin said.

They watched as Humungousaur jumped up, propelled by his powerful legs, and stomped down on the giant ball. It exploded into a cloud of alien chips.

"Puny chips!" Humungousaur bellowed.

Some of the chips fell to the ground, lifeless. The remaining chips regrouped, forming into six spiraling metal wheels covered in spikes. The new form didn't look all that impressive.

"That's kind of whatev," Kevin remarked.

The wheels careened toward Humungousaur. As they rolled, they sprayed out spike daggers at rapid speed. The sharp spikes flew in all directions.

"That's kind of a nightmare. Take cover!" Gwen yelled.

Gwen, Kevin, and Elena took shelter behind a concrete wall. Humungousaur kicked and punched the spike wheels out of the way. He smashed the daggers out of the air. Some of them made it past his fists, cutting into his skin. He winced, but kept on fighting.

The alien chips re-formed once again. This time they turned into one giant, spinning circle. They spun around Humungousaur's legs like a tornado, working their way up his body, covering him in a metal-spiked cocoon.

"It's got Ben!" Elena cried out, horrified.

Gwen was still hopeful. "That's easier said than done."

Boom! Humungousaur exploded from the top of the cocoon and landed with a thud next to Kevin's overturned car. The chips formed into a long, snake-like mass and flew at him.

"Oh no," Kevin said. "Don't do what I think you're gonna do."

Humungousaur picked up Kevin's car and held it above his head. He arched his back and hurled the car at the approaching mass of chips.

Bam! The spiky snake exploded into a hailstorm of dead chips. They rained to the ground, along with busted parts of Kevin's car.

Humungousaur walked through the smoke and wreckage. With each step, he transformed back into Ben.

"You did it, Ben!" Gwen cheered.

"That was so cool!" Elena cried.

"You destroyed my car!" Kevin yelled.

"What are you doing here?" Ben asked Gwen and Kevin.

"Well, I had a sudden urge to ship something overnight and suddenly we're up to our necks in your girlfriend's chips," Kevin said sarcastically. "And that's right about the time you come along and annihilate my car!"

"Those chips aren't mine," Elena protested. "I was trying to warn you."

Kevin looked at the mess around them. "Thanks. I'll consider myself warned."

He started to dig through the pieces of his car. Gwen turned to Ben.

"They're more than just autonomous tech," she said. "We found a hive of them at the Ship-It office, and they'd infected the clerk. Absorbed him."

"Yeah, we just ran into his extended family," Ben said, thinking of the zombies who attacked them. "They wanted to adopt us."

"We've got to get some of these active chips back to the lab right away," Gwen said.

Elena nodded. "Maybe they'll give us a clue about what happened to my father."

Kevin picked up a mangled bumper from his car. "Maybe we'll call and let you know, because you're not coming with us. You're trouble in a jug."

Elena wasn't intimidated. "Oh, I'm coming with you."

Gwen put her hands on her hips. "Ben, didn't Elena just lead you into a nest of techno-organic zombies?"

"She's coming," Ben said firmly. "One, she's in too much danger on her own now. And two . . . I trust her."

He looked Gwen directly in the eyes, staring her down. Elena smiled.

Kevin started to say something, but Elena took a card from her pocket and held it out to him.

"Speaking of which," she said.

"What's this?" Gwen asked.

"A very quick and trustworthy cab service," Elena told them.

She climbed onto the back of Ben's bike, and the two teens sped away.

CHAPTER NINE

Ben and Elena reached Plumbers HQ first. The place was buzzing with activity. Grandpa Max manned the main console in the lab. The faces of Plumbers from all around the world filled every data screen. They all talked at once, each in a different language.

Max spun around in his chair.

"Where in the Sam Hill has everyone been?" he barked. "I've got alien activity reports from installed Plumbers all over the globe!"

"Max, I—" Ben began.

"We're on priority alert," Max snapped. "You and I can sort out our differences later. And *she* stays in the brig." He nodded toward Elena.

"It's the chips. Validus's chips," Ben said.

Max frowned. "What? Did she tell you that?"

"It's true."

Gwen stepped into the room with Kevin. She held up a vial of the alien chips.

"The chips Validus stole have become active," she said.

"*Very* active," Kevin added.

Max knew he had to listen. Soon he was studying the chips under a powerful microscope.

"They're mobile, autonomous, resilient," he said, shaking his head. "These things were nothing but extra-terrestrial hardware. It's *impossible*."

"They also have a nasty habit of burrowing into people and taking over their minds," Ben told him.

Max's face was serious as he studied the readout on the computer screen.

"They've got an unusual energy signature. Can you use it to pinpoint them?" he asked.

"Already done," Kevin said. He moved to a nearby keyboard and started typing. A map of the globe appeared on the screens around them. Just like before, little red dots flashed to show where the chips were located. But now, there were ten times as many.

Everyone stared at the screens in disbelief.

"That's no hundred-mile radius," Kevin said.

"Millions of them," Ben breathed.

"And spreading at an increasing rate," Gwen added.

Elena looked triumphant. "So in other words, they *are* a threat! Just like my father said!"

Max stepped in front of her. "These things weren't alive three years ago. Your father's tinkering must have activated them. Now they pose a threat to the entire world."

Elena didn't back down. "You're wrong!" she shouted. "They were just hibernating. Just ask your know-it-all granddaughter."

"Stop it! Both of you!" Ben yelled. "Let's focus on solutions. Not blame."

Both Max and Elena knew he was right. They glared at each other, but quieted down.

"At least we know where they are," Gwen pointed out.

Kevin took an oversized Plumber's energy bazooka out of a nearby supply closet.

"Well, what are we waiting for?" he asked. "We've got a lot of shooting to do."

"What about the people who are already infected?" Elena asked.

Kevin pumped the barrel of the bazooka. "If it's

between the Ship-It clerk and me, I'm going to pick me."

Gwen shook her head. "No way. There's got to be another way."

Ben's eyes gleamed. He knew just what to do. "The queen!"

"What?" Max asked.

"That's right!" Elena said, excited. "The infected people, they all went on about their queen."

"Like the queen of an insect colony," Max said.

Kevin nodded. "In a bee hive or an ant hill, there's only one queen. She lays all the eggs, produces all the offspring, and tells everyone what to do."

Ben raised an eyebrow. Since when did Kevin know stuff?

Gwen caught his look. "The Science Channel," she explained.

"How do you destroy a hive?" Elena asked.

"You remove the queen," Ben explained. "The bees disband. The queen dies, the hive dies. We need to find the queen."

Max looked at Ben, impressed with his grandson. But there was no time for praise.

"Okay, nobody's getting any sleep tonight," he said. "I'm going to start dissecting these chips, see what they're made of. Kevin, we're going to need a more effective way to get past the drones."

Kevin sighed and put down the bazooka.

"Gwen, find a way to disrupt the connection between these things and their human hosts," Max instructed. Then he turned to Ben and Elena.

"Ben, there are a hundred million chips out there," he said. "Finding the queen is going to be like finding a needle in a haystack. Get on it. If Elena's here, she's gonna help, and I don't want her taking two steps without an escort."

Everyone paused for a second. This was one of the biggest alien threats to Earth they had ever faced.

"Come on, people!" Ben said. "Let's move!"

Everyone darted off to take care of the tasks Max had given them. Max picked up the active chips he had been studying under the microscope and put them back in the vial.

All except one chip, which wriggled free. It leapt onto Max's arm and crawled up to his neck. . . .

A few hours later, everyone was still working in the lab. Ben typed furiously on a keypad. Elena kept up the pace at a terminal beside him. Across the console, Gwen yawned as she typed. Next to her, Kevin was facedown on his keyboard, asleep.

"Gwen, why don't you get some shut-eye?" Ben suggested. "I need that brain of yours working if things get hot."

Gwen nodded sleepily. "Just for a few minutes. And you better wake me up."

Ben looked at Elena. "You too. Get some rest."

But Elena didn't slow down. "No chance. I'll sleep when my dad is home, safe and sound."

"Suit yourself," Ben said. He kept working.

Elena paused. "Thanks, Ben. For taking the risk to help me. For going against the team."

"Just like old times, right?" Ben said, trying to sound casual. "The guys didn't want you on the soccer team, and I stood up to them for you to join. You ended up being our MVP."

She eyed him. "You're not doing this for old times' sake."

"No, I'm doing this because I know what it's like. To be on your own, in a tough situation you never chose to be in," Ben said. He held up the Omnitrix on his wrist. "I didn't ask to be stuck with this. It just happened. And no one who isn't me knows how that feels."

Elena smiled. "I think I do."

Ben smiled back.

They worked until dawn. Ben got up from his chair, stretched, and headed into Max's office to give him a progress report.

"Kevin hasn't had any luck with the—"

The office was deserted. Ben tried the light switch, but the light didn't turn on.

"Max?" Ben called out.

He felt his way through the dark to Max's desk and turned on the lamp there. It wasn't very bright, but at least now he could see. He scanned the room, searching for signs of his grandfather.

Creeeeeeeeeeeeeak!

Ben heard the sound of a floorboard just behind him. Instinctively, he dodged out of the way. Spinning around, he saw Max with a metal box raised over his head. His eyes were glazed over.

"Max!" Ben yelled.

Max lunged after Ben, trying to hit him with the heavy box. Ben dodged out of the way again.

"Snap out of it! It's Ben!"

"We know," replied Max in a creepy voice.

Max tossed the box aside and tried to wrestle Ben to the ground. Ben pushed him away, but he was afraid to push too hard. He might be a zombie, but Max was still his grandfather.

"Hey, a little help in here!" Ben yelled.

Gwen, Kevin, and Elena rushed in.

"Max!" Gwen cried. "What's wrong with him?"

"I think he's having a little software issue," Ben said. "We've got to restrain him, but careful not to—"

As he spoke, Kevin put his hand on top of the metal desk, turning his arm to steel. He bonked Max on the head, and Max fell to the floor.

"—hurt him," Ben finished.

"What?" Kevin asked innocently. "He's restrained, isn't he?"

Gwen and Elena lifted up Max and put him in a chair. Gwen swiveled the desk lamp so that it shone in Max's eyes. The light reflected the tiny alien chips inside him.

"Max, are you okay?" Gwen asked.

"We're fine. Never better," Max said.

Ben, Gwen, Kevin, and Elena exchanged horrified looks. Max was talking like he was part of the hive.

"Why are you all looking at us like that?" Max asked. "We feel great. We're happy and we're going to colonize the Earth."

Kevin tried to lighten the mood. "He usually has a lot of odd jobs for us, but that one's new."

Gwen fought to hold back tears. "Oh, Grandpa . . ."

"Fight it, Max! Come on," Ben pleaded.

But Max was too far gone. While everyone was distracted, he began reaching for a control panel on his desk.

"You can't . . . stop what's coming," Max ranted. "The Plumbers are finished . . . mankind . . . finished."

Max pressed a button on the panel. Instantly, a smoky gas filled the room.

Taken by surprise, the kids coughed and tried to wave away the smoke.

When the smoke finally cleared, Max was gone!

CHAPTER TEN

Where did he go?" Elena asked.

"Nobody knows these tunnels like Max," Ben replied. "He's long gone by now."

Gwen frowned. "Now what?"

"Yeah, like it or not, the old man usually tells us what to do," Kevin said. "We need him."

"No we don't," Ben said firmly. "He needs us. We have to find this queen and stop her, or helping Max will be the least of our problems."

Ben sounded strong and decisive, and that was exactly what everyone needed. Gwen, Kevin, and Elena listened intently as he outlined his plan.

"Wherever this alien queen is, that's where we'll find

Elena's father *and* Max. We stop her, we stop the spread of these chips."

"And just how do you suggest we stop her?" Kevin asked.

Ben led them back to the lab. He turned on the big screens, and the world map showing the chip locations appeared on all of them. Ben stared at them for a while.

"Does anything seem weird to you guys about this map?" he asked.

"The color choices are a bit drab. Try sea foam blue," Kevin joked.

Gwen elbowed him in the gut. Ben pointed to the screens.

"Check out the concentration of chips. London, New York, Paris, Munich, and . . . central Missouri?"

Elena got it. "There are millions of people in all those cities, but that part of Missouri is . . ."

". . . the middle of nowhere," Kevin finished.

Gwen was already typing the name of the town into a search engine on her laptop.

"It's barely a town," she reported. "The only thing in Barren Rock, Missouri, is the world headquarters for Ship-It."

"Right," Ben said. "Those shipments from the local

Ship-It would have been the first wave of sentry soldiers. Now we're talking total immersion."

"And they need a big enough base to spread that many chips over the entire planet," Elena said, her eyes shining with excitement.

Gwen wasn't so sure. "Come on. They're taking over the world by twenty-four-hour shipping?"

"What's your brilliant theory?" Elena asked.

Gwen didn't reply. Ben and Elena's suggestion was far-fetched — but it was the only one that made sense.

"The plans I saw at Validus's lab looked like schematics for chip replication," Ben said. He pointed to Missouri on the map. "I think that's where the chips are being manufactured and distributed. And that's where we'll find the queen."

"Sounds like we're in for a road trip," Elena said.

"What do you mean 'we'?" Gwen snapped.

Ben shot her a look.

"Fine. She's coming," Gwen said reluctantly.

"Now, we just have to figure out how," Ben said. "With Kevin's car out of commission—"

A slow smile spread across Kevin's face. Ben looked puzzled.

"Follow me," Kevin said.

They left the Plumbers' lab and headed back up to Bellwood motors. The sun was up, and Big Ed was behind the desk. He led them to a tarp-covered car in the garage.

"Kevin built this for your birthday present," Big Ed told Ben.

"My birthday was two months ago," Ben said.

Kevin shrugged. "You can't rush genius."

He yanked off the tarp to reveal a wicked-looking green sportscar with black racing stripes.

Ben was speechless. For a second, he wondered if Kevin had been taken over by some alien force. The real Kevin was insulting, stubborn, and reckless. This was just . . . nice.

Gwen's eyes widened. "Oh my gosh, Kevin. It's beautiful," she said.

"*She*. She's beautiful," Kevin corrected her. "You call a car 'she.' And you're right. Don't be jealous. You've got good qualities, too."

Elena couldn't believe what Kevin had done for Ben. She'd been living in hiding with her dad for three years. She had almost forgotten what it was like to have friends.

"A car. Your friend built you a car," she said softly.

"The weapons and defense systems aren't online, but she'll run," Big Ed told them.

"Fact is, she'll pretty much eat anything in her path," Kevin said proudly.

"I don't know what to say," Ben said finally. "I can't wait to try her out."

Kevin shook his head. "Oh, you're not driving. I said I was going to give you the car. That was before you bailed out on the team. I'm keeping her."

Ben was relieved to hear Kevin acting normal.

"Oh, I'm driving," Ben said confidently.

"How do you figure?" Kevin asked.

"Humungousaur would be happy to *throw* the car to Missouri," Ben said with a triumphant smile.

Hours later, the four of them were speeding down the highway with Ben at the wheel. They kept going until they reached Barren Rock, Missouri. Ben parked the car at a rocky hilltop overlooking the town, and everyone climbed out.

Gwen shivered. "Missouri in February. It's my dream vacation. Only forty degrees colder."

"This place makes the Null Void feel like Miami Beach," Kevin agreed.

They crouched down behind a boulder. Ben produced a pair of binoculars, and they took turns looking through them. Down below was the massive, sprawling complex of buildings that housed the Ship-It headquarters. Eighteen-wheel trucks were leaving the hub, heading in all directions. On the loading bays, zombified workers loaded waiting trucks with wooden crates.

"The people. They're all infected," Gwen said in a hushed voice.

A worker driving a forklift loaded a truck with a pallet of crates. One of the crates fell over, spilling chips onto the pavement below.

"Whoops! That's coming out of your zombie paycheck," Kevin joked.

Gwen shook her head as the seriousness of the situation hit her.

"All those crates are filled with chips," she said.

"There must be millions," Elena put in.

"Probably six billion," Ben said. "That's how many people there are on Earth. Okay, let's get inside."

They made their way down to the complex. The wide

front entrance was strangely empty, probably because all the workers were busy loading trucks.

Ben laid out his plan. "Our first priority is to find the queen. That'll put a stop to any more chip manufacturing. And I think she's our best shot at freeing all the infected people, Max included."

Slowly, the four teens made their way to an outdoor loading dock. The place was crawling with zombies loading a truck. Ben and the others hid behind a forklift, trying not to get noticed. But being around all those zombies was nerve-wracking. The workers sealed the truck doors, and then walked right past them.

Elena pointed to an entrance on the other side of the loading dock. Zombie workers were making their way out of it down a ramp.

"Looks like that's where we want to be, right in there," she said.

"Oh no!" Gwen cried.

She pointed to the next loading dock. A zombie worker was driving a forklift. It was Grandpa Max!

"Grandpa," Gwen said softly.

She started to run toward him, but Ben held her back. He pulled her behind a large crate, where they hid with Kevin and Elena.

"No, Gwen," Ben warned. "If he sees us, he'll alert the others that we don't belong here. Hive mind. He's one of them now. It's up to us."

It was too dangerous to walk around openly now. They ducked inside and headed for the heart of the complex. They climbed up on the catwalk, the crisscrossed network of platforms underneath the ceiling. From there, they could spy on the workers without being seen.

The center of the Ship-It complex was filled with workers and crates. Hundreds of zombies worked at long conveyor belts, filling up boxes with chips.

"It's like a human assembly line," Gwen whispered.

Ben nodded. "No sign of her highness, the queen. But there's someone we *do* know."

Kevin followed his gaze. "It's the chip off the old block from back at the mill."

The mysterious man in the trenchcoat was standing on top of a large platform. He wasn't wearing his hat this time, and he had his back to them. Cables ran from his body down to the platform.

He turned around to direct a group of workers, and Ben and the others could clearly see his face for the first time, the same face from Max's computer screen.

"It's Victor Validus!" Gwen cried.

Kevin was angry. He pointed at Elena. "I knew it! I told you not to trust her!"

"It's not like that!" Elena protested.

"You knew all along that your father was behind this," Gwen accused.

"It's not his fault," Elena said. "My father would never do anything evil!"

Ben felt betrayed. "You said you didn't know this guy!"

"I *don't*," Elena insisted, and she meant it. "That's not my dad. He's become some kind of freak!"

"You're both in it together," Kevin said. "It's a trap!"

He touched the nearest steel beam and armored up

his right arm, ready to attack Elena. Ben put an arm in front of him.

"Back off! It's okay," he said.

"Yeah? How is this okay?" Kevin asked.

"Ben, her father is controlling the chips," Gwen pointed out. "He's orchestrating the whole operation!"

"Is he? Looks to me like the chips are controlling him, just like they are Grandpa Max. It's not a trap," Ben said calmly.

But when he turned to Elena, his face was filled with sadness. He knew she hadn't told him the whole truth. She'd known her father was infected all along. "I trusted you, Elena," he said.

Elena looked miserable. "I had to lie. I knew you'd react like this! Treat me like the enemy. Refuse to help me. Just like the Plumbers did with my father!"

"Then I guess you don't know us as well as you thought." He looked at Kevin and Gwen. "Right?"

Kevin and Gwen were quiet. Ben was right. If they had known the truth from the start, they would have wanted to help Elena. Why should that change now? They couldn't refuse to help someone in need.

"I'm sorry. I truly am," Elena said sincerely. "I just wanted this nightmare to end."

"Well, it looks like it's just beginning," Gwen said. "I think we found out how they're making the chips."

She pointed at the platform Validus was standing on. Piles of chips surrounded him. Workers shoveled them into carts and wheeled them off onto conveyor belts. A closer look revealed something incredible — the chips were traveling through tubes connected to his body. The living chips were growing on his skin and then making their way into the tubes.

"No way," Kevin said.

Elena looked like she might cry. "Daddy!"

Ben, Elena, Gwen, and Kevin quickly moved off the catwalk, away from the center of the action. They huddled together in one of the tunnels extending from the hub and began to discuss their next move.

"That's what those plans were for," Ben told them. "He was conducting tests on himself. He's the hive. His own body is producing them by the thousands."

Gwen looked serious. "In a colony, only the queen can reproduce, so . . ."

"The queen is inside my dad!" Elena realized.

"We gotta shut him down, Ben," Kevin said. "Destroy him, destroy the queen."

"No, you can't!" Elena cried.

"I'm sorry, Elena, but Kevin may be right," Gwen said matter-of-factly. "I know it's hard, but if it's a choice between one man and the human race . . ."

Elena gave Ben a pleading look. "You said you'd save him! It's not his fault! He's the only family I have."

Kevin made his case. "Dude, I know it's hard, but unless you take out this guy, the whole world falls. You *know* what Max would do."

Ben took a deep breath and tried to think.

Like it or not, the Omnitrix was part of him. The final decision was up to him. Save Elena's father, or save the world? Was the choice really so black-and-white?

"I don't know what Max would do," he said finally. "But I know what I wouldn't do. I don't destroy victims. I save them."

"Man, this isn't the time for do-good heroics!" Kevin yelled in frustration.

"This *is* the time for you to stop yelling!" Gwen whispered. "Like now!"

"Too late for that," Elena warned.

A zombie worker at the end of the tunnel was staring at them suspiciously. Because all the workers were connected by the hive mind, every worker in the place turned toward the tunnel. The kids froze.

A small group of zombie workers headed down the tunnel. That was it—their cover was blown.

Elena, Gwen, and Kevin turned to Ben.

"Okay, so now it's safe to yell," Kevin said. "What the heck are you gonna do, Ben?"

Ben started dialing choices on the Omnitrix.

Gwen looked concerned. "Ben, wait a minute!" she said. "What do we do if Humungousaur or Alien X gets absorbed by the hive? It's all over."

As Gwen spoke, a mysterious new hologram popped up from the Omnitrix. Ben stared at it, mulling over Gwen's words.

"Absorbed by the hive . . . is pretty much what I had in mind," Ben told her.

The zombies moved closer. Kevin touched a metal beam and armored up.

Ben showed the hologram to the others. "Remember when the Omnitrix scanned the chips' DNA? I can fight them from the inside . . . if I *become* one of them! The watch has been cooking this up all along. Time to take it out of the oven."

Ben raised his other hand to slap the Omnitrix, but Kevin grabbed his wrist.

"Ben, this isn't anything like you've become before," he warned.

"Kevin's right," Gwen agreed. "It's a hive-mind-based organism."

"So?" Ben asked.

"I think the Omnitrix can turn you into one of these things, but I don't know if it can keep you in control once it does. You may become a permanent slave to the hive," she explained.

"A turbo-charged, killer-weapon slave," Kevin added.

Elena was distraught. "Ben, no! I don't want to lose you too!"

Ben paused. "We're out of options. I'm gonna have to put my faith in the Omnitrix."

Overcome with emotion, Gwen shoved her cousin. "It always has to be your way, doesn't it, Ben? Just like walking out on the Plumbers!"

Ben shook his head. "Okay, so maybe I should've stayed and talked it out. But this is different."

"Why?" Gwen asked.

"This is something I *don't* want to do," he replied. "I just don't see any other way."

Suddenly, four zombies appeared out of nowhere and

grabbed Elena. She screamed as they started to drag her down the tunnel.

"Elena!" Ben yelled.

Elena wrenched her arms free, grabbed a long metal pipe, and started swinging at the zombies. They scattered like bowling pins. Kevin, Gwen, and Ben formed a small circle back to back so they could fight in all directions.

But the zombies were the least of their worries. A swarm of chips crawled toward them, covering the floor, walls, and ceiling. In minutes, they would be overcome by the sheer number of them.

"What are we supposed to do?" Gwen asked.

"Keep them busy!" Ben shouted.

"How?" Gwen asked.

Ben slammed his palm down on the Omnitrix.

"I trust you," he said.

Ben glowed green as the new organism fused with his DNA. When the transformation was complete, Ben looked down at his body. He looked exactly the same.

"What?" Ben wondered.

Then he looked up—and saw a huge pair of sneakers in front of him. He looked farther up, and saw Kevin and Gwen towering over him like giants.

Ben realized what had happened. "I'm . . . small!"

CHAPTER TWELVE

Ben quickly began to change. Plates of metal armor sprouted all over his body. The pieces of armor looked like the alien chips. They covered every inch of his skin except for his back. Two antennae grew from his head. Metal wings formed on his back.

"Not too shabby!" said Ben's new alien form.

He flexed his arms, and arcs of electricity shot from his body. Kevin and Gwen couldn't see Ben, but the sparks got their attention.

"What is that?" Kevin asked.

"He's turned into some kind of nano-mechanical organism," Gwen realized. "Just like the chips!"

"Nanomech! I like it!" Ben cried.

Nanomech raced through the crowd of zombies, heading right for Validus. He darted between the zombies' giant shoes as he ran.

"Hey, I'm walking here!" Nanomech yelled.

Nanomech broke into a run and leapt into the air. His wings spread out, and he soared over the heads of the giant zombies.

"Time to get even smaller." He somersaulted in the air, growing smaller and smaller each time he tumbled. Soon he was even smaller than an alien chip. He flew right toward Validus's face. The man's nostrils loomed before him like two huge caverns.

Validus swatted at Nanomech. He shrunk even more—and flew right into a nostril!

"Oh man . . . this is gross!" Nanomech yelled.

If the queen was controlling Validus, she had probably taken up residence inside his brain. He flew up the nostril and entered Validus's brain canal.

He immediately encountered a storm of brain matter. It reminded him of flying in space through a meteor storm. He dodged particles as he made his way to a neuronal pathway. Perfect! He traveled through the corridor of neurons and emerged in the middle of a nerve center.

Electricity fired around him. Sitting in the center

of a crackling nucleus was a strange alien figure. Like Nanomech, she looked humanoid, but she was covered with metal armor.

She spoke, but her voice sounded like an electronic buzz. Nanomech's antennae moved to properly tune her in.

"Listen to my voice . . . inside your head . . . you must obey," the queen intoned in a hypnotic tone.

Nanomech shook his antennae. He had to get the voice out of his head. If he fell under the queen's control, all would be lost.

"You are one of us now, Ben Tennyson," the queen said. "You're no longer like these humans. You're better. How can you care about their problems when the universe is yours? Join me."

"No . . ." Nanomech said, straining to resist.

Back in the warehouse, Gwen and Kevin worked together to rescue Elena from the zombies. Gwen shot blasts of pink energy at the alien chip swarm, pushing the chips back. Metal Kevin was picking up zombies like they were rag dolls and tossing them to the side.

They quickly reached Elena. Gwen grabbed her.

"Where is Ben? What is he doing?" Elena asked.

"Whatever it is, it isn't working," Gwen said.

A group of zombies rushed toward them.

Wham! Gwen blasted them with alien energy.

Bam! Elena whacked one with a pipe.

Slam! Kevin picked up one in each arm and threw them across the room. They collided with the platform Validus stood on. Victor Validus tried to steady his balance as the battle raged on inside his head. . . .

Nanomech was feeling woozy. He was starting to fall under the queen's spell.

"You're different from these other drones. Stronger," she told him. "You can be my king."

Nanomech concentrated with every ounce of strength he had.

Zap! He blasted the queen with a bolt of electricity. A look of shock appeared on her alien face.

"Sorry. I'm just not ready for a serious commitment like that," Nanomech said.

The queen recovered quickly.

Zap! Zap! Zap! She fired a barrage of bolts at Nanomech. They sizzled around his armor, trying to get inside his body and control him. Nanomech shrugged them off and advanced toward her.

"Impossible!" the queen fumed.

Long tendrils of energy snaked from her body. Her whole form crackled with electric power.

"Then you'll die with the humans!"

BAM! She hurled a huge, glowing energy ball at Nanomech. The blast knocked him off his feet.

"You were a fool to transform into a drone chip. I can easily defeat any puny drone," the queen said.

Jagged streaks of electricity shot from her body, lighting up the nerve center like a fireworks show.

Nanomech held up his arms to shield himself from the energy. "But I'm not just any drone," he said, struggling to rise from his feet. "You said it yourself. I'm half-drone . . . half-human."

Nanomech stood tall. Tendrils of electricity sprouted from his back. They glowed brighter and grew longer than the queen's tendrils.

"Drones can adapt. And humans . . . NEVER. GIVE. UP!"

Nanomech hurled a massive electric blast at the queen.

BOOM!

The queen exploded into a million pieces.

CHAPTER
THIRTEEN

Victor Validus staggered and fell to his knees.

All around the warehouse, the zombie workers stopped in their tracks. The canisters of alien chips exploded in a rippling cloud of dust and smoke. Streams of golden energy flew out of the mouths of the stunned workers.

Boom! The golden energy exploded overhead. All of the power in the complex went out, plunging everything into darkness. Then the main cargo door opened up, flooding the place with sunlight.

Validus stood up. He looked dazed and groggy, but like his old self again.

"Daddy!" Elena cried happily. She turned to Kevin and Gwen. "He's all right!"

"Elena?" Validus asked. He looked at the chaos around him. "What on Earth . . ."

The workers slowly regained their senses. They stumbled around the warehouse, shaky and confused. Ben raced through them and stepped behind Elena. Kevin and Gwen were locked in a celebratory hug.

"What am I? Chopped liver?" Ben asked. "Hello? I just saved the world. *Again*."

"Don't look at me," Kevin said. "I'm not hugging you."

Smiling, Elena rushed to Ben and wrapped her arms around him.

Ben blushed, embarrassed. "Actually, you may not want to hug me so tightly. I flew through a lot of snot."

They all laughed. Then Ben remembered something.

"Max!"

He took off through the crowd, shoving his way through the sea of people in search of his grandfather.

"Max? Where are you? Max!" he yelled.

A large hand grabbed Ben and pulled him out of the crowd.

"You had a lot of gall. Disobeying orders!" Max barked angrily. "Defying my authority!"

"Grandpa, I—"

"You know what that kind of behavior gets you?" Max asked.

Ben braced himself for bad news. He'd probably lose his Plumbers' badge or—

But Max gripped him in a bear hug. Ben smiled.

It felt good.

As the sun set over the Ship-It center, hundreds of ex-zombies poured out of the complex. They talked to each other and shared cell phones in an attempt to figure out what was going on.

In their midst were Ben, Gwen, Kevin, and Elena. Max followed them, supporting Victor Validus. Elena's father looked like he had been through a lot.

"I'm sorry, Victor," Max told his old friend. "None of this would ever have happened if I'd trusted you."

"No, Max," Validus said, his voice weak. "It wasn't right to go it alone and allow myself to be taken over by the hive queen." He turned to Ben. "Thank you, Ben. I am forever in your debt."

"It's your daughter you should be thanking," Ben said. "If it wasn't for Elena, I'd be at a school football game right now."

Elena smiled shyly. "He's just being modest."

"Ben, modest? Impossible," Kevin said.

Ben grinned at his friends. "I guess we are a pretty good team."

"We're a *great* team," Elena said.

"We're more than that. We're Plumbers," Gwen said. She beamed at Max. "And the Plumbers have a great leader."

"Indeed they do," Max said. He put a hand on Ben's shoulder. "Ben, what would you say if I ask you to step in?"

Ben was startled. "What?"

"I'm not getting any younger," Max went on. "Believe me, I've been waiting long enough for this moment."

Ben shook his head. "I couldn't take over."

"You kinda already did," Max pointed out. "You're ready, Ben. Fact is, the Omnitrix could've ended up on anybody's wrist. We oughta count ourselves lucky it found its way to you." His eyes gleamed with pride as he looked at his grandson.

"Hate to say it, but Max is right," Gwen agreed.

Kevin wasn't as enthusiastic. "Can we get, like, a thirty-day trial period?"

Gwen elbowed him in the ribs.

"Well, my first order of business will be to un-accept

Max's resignation," Ben said. "You're not getting out that easily," he told his grandfather.

"That may be true," Max admitted. He scanned the large parking lot. "Where in blazes did that zombie-me put my ride?"

Ben grinned and headed for his brand new car. Elena and Gwen fell in step behind him.

"What did you mean 'we're a great team'?" Gwen asked Elena. "You're not on the team."

"I am, Red," Elena said. "I earned my place and I suggest you move your locker far from mine because—"

"Oh, I don't think so!" Gwen replied.

Kevin put an arm around Ben. "Better get used to it. That's the sound of things to come," he said. "Now, give me back my car keys."

"Nice try, Kev, but from now on, I'm driving," Ben told him.

Kevin paused. Then he burst into a run. "I call shotgun!" he yelled.

The four of them climbed into the car. A moment later, Ben was driving off into the setting sun.

Tomorrow, the world might need saving again. But for now, it was time to go home.